SECRET SANTA FOR GRUMPY ELVES

AN OBSCURE ACADEMY STORY

LAURA GREENWOOD

BLURB

Holly the elf doesn't normally enjoy the Christmas season, but all that changes when her flatmates insist on exchanging Secret Santa gifts.

On her quest to find the perfect present, Holly meets a fellow elf who is determined to make sure she has some fun, no matter what it takes.

As sparks start to fly between them, Holly finds herself looking forward to spending more time with Chris, even if it means celebrating the Holidays.

-

Secret Santa For Grumpy Elves is a light-hearted elf academy m/f romance set at Obscure Academy. It is Chris and Holly's complete story.

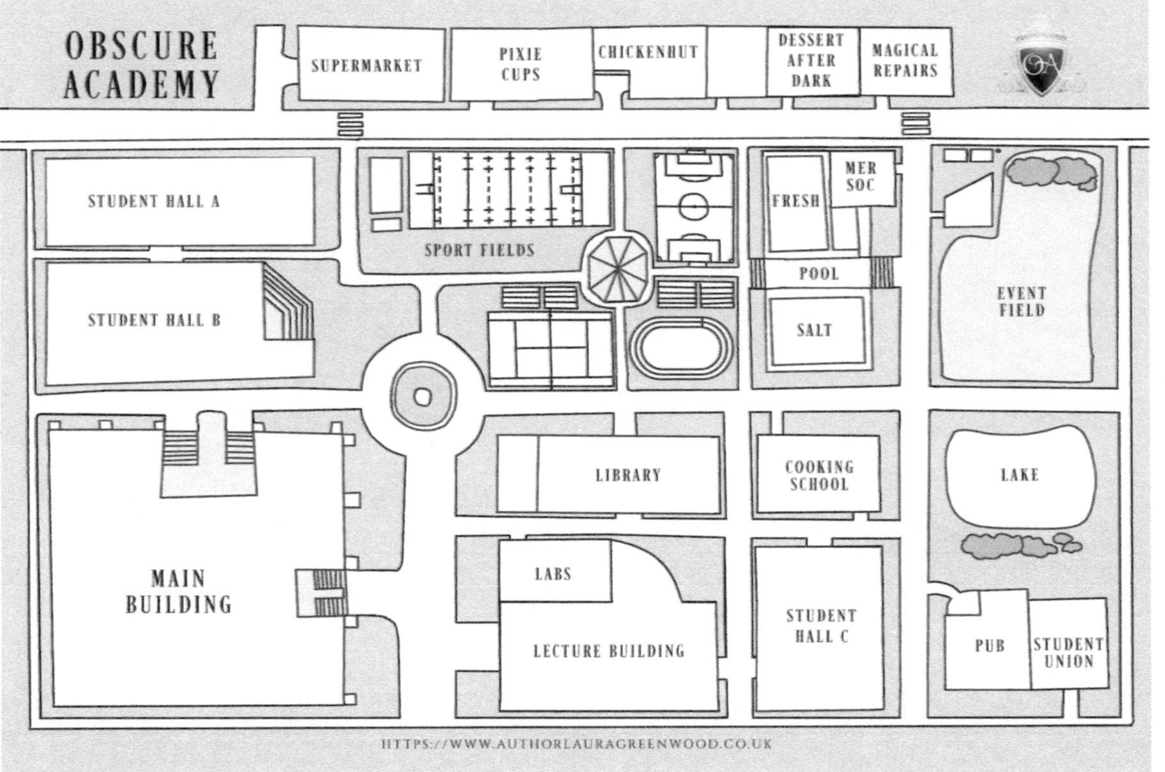

OBSCURE ACADEMY
SUPERMARKET
PIXIE CUPS
CHICKENHUT
DESSERT AFTER DARK
MAGICAL REPAIRS
STUDENT HALL A
STUDENT HALL B
SPORT FIELDS
FRESH
MER SOC
POOL
SALT
EVENT FIELD
MAIN BUILDING
LIBRARY
COOKING SCHOOL
LAKE
LABS
LECTURE BUILDING
STUDENT HALL C
PUB
STUDENT UNION
HTTPS://WWW.AUTHORLAURAGREENWOOD.CO.UK

ONE

HOLLY

MUSIC BLARES FROM THE SPEAKERS, filling the whole shopping centre with a false sense of holiday cheer. I wish they wouldn't bother. They should keep to the same kind of music as they normally do. It's still falsely happy, but at least it doesn't force fake happiness in the season on those of us who would rather not celebrate at all.

I tuck a strand of hair behind my ear before thinking better of it. Any other month, I wouldn't care about people seeing the pointiness at the top, but this is different. Christmas brings out the worst in people when it comes to dealing with the fae, especially elves.

Not that most humans are able to tell the difference between us by sight. Most supernaturals probably can't either.

I tug the strands back out and cover up my ears. I should get myself a nice woolly hat to cover them up with. At least that won't end up in small children running up to me and begging me to tell them what Santa has got them for Christmas.

Despite many attempts to rectify the image, we still seem to get associated with the North Pole. To my knowledge, no elves have ever lived there. It's too cold for any of our likings.

I push the thoughts aside and focus on the task at hand. My flat has insisted on doing Secret Santa along with our Christmas dinner before term ends, and while I may not be a huge fan of the season, I do like my flatmates and I want them to continue to like me.

The sickly sweet scent of the soap store I know Grace likes attacks me even before I turn the corner and find it. But at least I know I'm heading to where I'm supposed to be.

"Good afternoon, welcome to Aroma," a cheery guy says as I step through the door and into the offensive store. "How can we help you this Christmas time?"

"Aren't you supposed to use holiday?" I mutter.

He just smiles. "Don't I know you? I think I've seen you in my economics class, at Obscure Academy, right?"

I look more closely and imagine him without the tiny red hat and the matching t-shirt complete with printed bells around a green collar. I cock my head to the side, but can't decide whether I've seen him before. "Maybe."

"Ah, so you are in the economics class."

"That's not hard to guess, a lot of people take economics and I'm the right age to be attending Obscure," I point out.

"True. I'm Chris."

"Holly," I respond without thinking about it.

"That's a nice name."

"No comment about how it's good for the season?" I raise an eyebrow.

Chris chuckles. "I thought you might be bored of that observation."

A small snort escapes me. "You're not wrong there."

"What brings you to Aroma?"

"I have to get a Secret Santa gift for one of my flatmates."

"Ah, you're doing that too."

"I imagine a lot of people are."

"Of course, we're all broke."

"You have a job," I point out.

"Mmhmm. The only way I can afford the nights out." He winks at me.

Despite my overall dissatisfaction with the season, I find myself warming to Chris. He has one of those personalities that makes it difficult to be annoyed in his presence. I glance at his hairline, wanting to see if there's any hint of a pointy ear. Elves have a way of making people feel at ease if they want to. I've never used it to get a job in retail before, but I can see how it might be helpful when dealing with a difficult customer. Unfortunately, his hair covers his ears too well for me to be sure about whether or not he's an elf too.

"Anyway, I was thinking about a soap gift set or something? My flatmate never stops talking about this place. She's sure there's magic in the soap or something."

"I'm afraid I'll have to disappoint her on that front. The only magic in these formulas is science."

"You could argue that science is just magic of another kind," I point out.

He laughs. "That's fair. Do you know what her favourite scent is?"

I shake my head. "She always smells a bit fruity to me."

"Ah, then I think we have the perfect gift basket. Follow me." He leads me deeper into the store.

I glance over my shoulder in time to see one of the other members of staff taking his place at the entrance to help the next shopper find what they need. It must be an exhausting job. I can't imagine interacting with people so much.

"Here we go. It's the Tutti Frutti gift basket." He gestures to a shelf filled with three different sized baskets.

"It's an original name," I comment dryly.

His lips quirk into a real smile, but he covers it quickly with what I have to assume is his cheerier customer service one. "We don't have any input into the names."

"I know. And I guess it tells me what's in it."

"What's your Secret Santa budget?"

"Ten pounds."

He lets out a low whistle. "Your flat is going all out. My friends decided that we're going to do Pound Secret Santa."

"Let's guess, your budget is a pound?"

"More than that, we have to get the gift from one of the pound shops. There's even going to be a prize for the tackiest." He picks up the smallest gift basket and hands it to me.

"That actually sounds kind of fun," I admit.

"If you get the right person, it is. Get the wrong person, and they end up insulted because you get them a toy kitchen."

"Because they can't cook?" Amusement dances in my voice.

"Exactly. That's the gift basket you need. It's eight quid, but the medium one is twelve."

I nod. "I'll just add some chocolates or something."

"You're not tempted by the toy kitchen?" A boyish grin stretches over his face.

"I don't think she'll see the funny side of it." At all. I like Grace, but her sense of humour is about as flexible as an iron fence. Not that I've been near many of them to know exactly what that's like. An iron allergy is something not to be messed with.

"Hmmm, best to avoid it then."

"Thanks for your help. I'll just take this to the till." I gesture in that direction, lingering for a moment, though I'm not sure why. "Would you like to get a drink with me?" I blurt.

"I thought you'd never ask."

"Then why didn't you?"

"It's hard to tell when someone's just being extra

nice because they know retail jobs around Christmas suck extra hard, or if they're actually interested."

A bemused laugh comes from me. "Maybe the drink is just me being extra nice too."

"But it's still a free drink." He winks at me. "I finish at five. Do you want to meet at the Campus pub at seven? I hear there's a pub quiz going on tonight."

"You want to do a pub quiz with someone you just met?"

"How someone behaves in a competitive setting can tell you a lot about someone," he points out. "And I've been wanting to go all term, but my friends refuse to go with me for some reason."

"All right. Seven it is. Prepare to be impressed by my vast knowledge of the world." Where is this coming from? I'm not normally so forward unless I've had a drink or five. There's just something about him that makes me want to get to know him more. And there isn't any harm in getting a drink. The campus pub will have too many witnesses for anything to go weirdly wrong anyway.

I head towards the till and pay for my purchase, satisfied that I have a decent present for Grace while trying not to linger on which of my flatmates has me. I hope they err on the side of useful when they buy for me rather than just getting me a tenner's worth of chocolate. Though that could have its uses too, especially if my drink with Chris goes badly.

I wave at him as I walk out of the shop, feeling a lot more upbeat than when I entered. I can try and pretend that it's just because I've hunted down the perfect present, but I know that's not the case.

TWO

CHRIS

I HOPE HOLLY DOESN'T MIND that I suggested The Red Phoenix as the place for us to have our first date. While a busy pub isn't great for being able to hear all of the conversation, I'm hoping it will make her feel safe to be around so many people. The last thing I want is to scare her away before we've even started properly dating.

"I had no idea pub quiz night was so popular," she half-shouts in my direction.

"Me neither." And if I'd known it was going to be this busy, I might have thought of an alternative. "What do you want to drink?"

"This is my round, you said you were only coming for the free drink," she points out.

I laugh lightly, remembering that I did in fact say that. "I'm not going to say no to that."

"What do you want?" she asks.

"Cider is good."

"From the tap? I saw a good still one over there." She gestures towards the bar. Not that I can see past the crowd of people gathered around it. Even this close, I can't make out anything.

"That sounds good to me. Though I don't mind the fruity ones that come in bottles either," I admit.

"They'll do in a pinch." Somehow, she manages to get the attention of one of the bartenders and he gets us our drinks quickly. Which is more of a relief than I want to admit. I don't want to spend time with all the people here, I want to spend time with her.

"Shall we? I saw a table over there." I wave towards the section that's set aside for the pub quiz, grateful that the tables haven't all filled up yet.

I dig a few coins out of my pocket and drop them into the jar being held by the rope monitor so he'll let us through.

"I feel so fancy," Holly whispers.

"It's the rope, isn't it?" I smile at her, feeling the same even though I know it's just a rope.

We take a seat at one of the tables. Just in time, it seems, as others seem to have had the same thought about getting ready for the quiz.

"We need a good team name," I say.

"Is Holly and Chris not good enough?" she suggests.

I raise an eyebrow. "Shouldn't that be alphabetical?"

Amusement dances in her eyes. "It can be if you want."

"Or we combine them. Which do you think is better, Cholly, or Holis."

A loud snort of amusement escapes from her, but she doesn't seem phased. "Holis, definitely."

"Cholly it is then." I give her an exaggerated wink and scribble it down on the page.

"That makes me half want to lose on purpose so it doesn't get read out in front of everyone," she jokes.

"At least it's memorable. Isn't that better than having a name like let's get quizzical read out?"

"Fair point." She takes a sip of her cider and lets out a satisfied sigh. "That's good."

"Oh?" I take a drink of my own, enjoying the sweet tartness of the drink. "It is. I might end up coming back here just for this."

"It's so hard to get good cider in a pub these days," she says.

"What got you on to drinking it? I don't know a lot of girls who choose to have a pint. Especially not on a date." Oops, maybe not the best thing to say. I don't want her to feel like I'm judging her choice of drink.

"I never really thought about it being a bad date drink," she mumbles.

"I'm sorry, that wasn't a good question for me to ask. I don't think it's a bad date drink. I picked it too." I gesture to my pint. "I'm not very good at the whole dating thing."

"You're not doing too bad," she assures me.

"Maybe you're just as bad and aren't noticing?"

"That could be it, I've not been on many dates."

"And yet you asked me," I point out.

"That was a spur of the moment thing," she responds. "I'm not even sure what made me do it."

"Well I'm glad you did," I say decisively. She's easy to be around, more so than a lot of people I've spent time with, even when not on dates.

"Me too." She pushes a strand of hair behind her ear, the slight point at the top the only hint of what she is. If I wasn't looking for it, I'd probably never guess she was an elf.

"Good evening everyone, please take your seats for tonight's pub quiz, we'll start in five minutes," the announcer says over the loudspeaker.

"Are you ready to prove to everyone that we're the best?" I ask.

"Aren't we at a disadvantage with just the two of us?"

"That depends what your quiz skills are like. But don't they say it's the taking part that counts?"

"That's said by people who don't know how fun winning is," she counters, seeming to be enjoying herself as much as I am.

A loud laugh bursts from me. "All right, then let's try to win."

"What do we win?"

"A free drink, I think. Nothing fancy."

"Ah, so that was your plan. We'll have to use the free drinks tonight and suddenly our date is extended."

"You caught me." That's a lie. I honestly didn't think about that, I just thought it would be a good way of making sure she didn't feel like I was coming on too intensely. "Okay, I have a good first date question."

"Hit me with it."

"What's the worst thing about being an elf?"

Her eyebrows shoot upwards. "You're heading straight for that when I don't even know what you are?"

I push my own hair back, revealing the tell-tale point of an ear. I'm sure she's already worked it out from things I've said, but it's good to confirm it. "I'm an elf too."

"So you mean other than the fact everyone wants to ask us what's happening at the North Pole all the time?" she checks.

"Yes, that one's a given."

"The lack of cool magic. Everyone around us can do all this amazing stuff and we're stuck with being charismatic? That kind of sucks," she says.

"Except that charisma can get you far in life."

"Maybe." She doesn't sound convinced, but she also doesn't seem too bothered about it.

"Attention everyone," the announcer says, cutting our conversation short. "The quiz is about to begin."

I ready myself to start writing down answers while Holly takes another sip of her drink.

"The first round is nature," he says. "Question one..."

The questions come in quick succession, only just allowing us enough time to scribble down the answer before the announcer moves on to the next one.

"Question ten, the last question before we go on to the next round."

"What do you think the next one is going to be?" she whispers to me.

"Hopefully not geography, I always suck at that round."

"I'm hit and miss with it too."

Then we'd really better hope that it isn't that.

"What male animal is the one to carry its young?" He repeats the question a couple of times to make sure everyone in the room has heard it.

"I know this one," she whispers excitedly.

I hand her the pen, letting our fingers brush against one another as she takes it. There's a small hitch in her breathing, as if she's extra aware of the contact.

She clears her throat and scribbles seahorse on the answer sheet.

I nod, remembering something vaguely familiar about the fact. "Ah, yes, I remember seeing a documentary about that."

"Is it cool to admit you like watching nature shows?" she asks.

"Nothing is cooler than gaining more knowledge," I respond. "But I'm also not looking to impress you with how cool I am. I'm trying to impress you with my real personality."

A genuine smile stretches over her face. "It's working."

"I'm glad to hear it." And relieved.

"Our next round is history," the announcer says.

"How are you on this one?" she asks.

"Not too bad so long as it's all British stuff. I might be a bit more stuck if they start asking about the American revolution."

"Noted. We'll just have to guess at those answers." She sits back and waits for the announcer to continue.

The questions come thick and fast, but we seem to field most of them well enough.

"Round five," the announcer says. "This is the final one and its general knowledge. If anyone needs me to repeat a question from the previous round, now is the chance."

"How are we doing so far?" she asks me.

"Pretty good." I certainly don't think we're going to need any repeated questions. "The only one we haven't finished putting an answer for is question six from the history round."

"What was that one again?"

"The name of the last king of France. We've just written Louis." Somehow, I doubt that's going to be the winning answer.

"Are you sure it isn't Louis XVI? That sounds right to me."

I shake my head. "He's the last king before the revolution, but they brought the monarchy back after that."

"How do you know so much about French history?"

"I did a France since the revolution module last term. It was interesting, but I don't think I've retained much of it." Which says a lot about how useful the information is.

"And not at the right time either."

"Clearly not," I agree.

"What if we put Louis XVII?" she suggests.

"I don't think that's right, but it's better than nothing." I scribble it down.

"Question one of the general knowledge round," the announcer says, pulling us out of our conversation. "True or false, a man has eaten a whole Cessna 150 plane before, without using magic."

Holly raises an eyebrow. "What do you think?"

"I have no idea. It sounds so far-fetched that it's got to be true. But at the same time, how?"

"A quirk of nature? Or maybe there was magic involved but no one realised?"

She might be onto something there. "That could

be it, I can't pretend to understand supernatural genetics."

"I don't think anyone does."

"So what do you think, true or false?"

"Put down true." The way she says it makes me think that she's certain it'll pay off. It'll be interesting to see if it does.

The next question takes us off guard with how long it took us to answer the first one. We do our best to pay more attention, especially as we both seem to be confident in our chances of actually winning.

"And the final question, the highest value Canadian heist wasn't for money, what was it for?" the announcer asks.

"Is it bad that I want to say maple syrup?" she quips.

I let out a low chuckle. "That's what it's going to be, isn't it?"

"The chances are high. That stuff is expensive."

"All right, maple syrup it is." I don't have any idea if it's the right answer, but it could be. "Any other questions we want to go back to?"

Holly shakes her head. "I think that's it."

"All right, I'll go hand this in. Do you want another drink?" I gesture to her empty pint glass.

"Sure. Same again?".

I nod and get to my feet. "I'll be right back."

I make my way over to the bar, handing in our answer sheet as I pass the announcer. When I get to the bar, I twist myself around to make sure that Holly's going to be able to see the drinks I get the entire time. I know I'm not going to put anything in them, but she barely knows me still, and it's important that she can see.

I wave at her and she lifts her hand to return it, filling me with hope that our date is going as well for her as it is for me.

The bar isn't as crowded as before, and it's only a couple of minutes before I get two new pints of cider put down in front of me. With them in hand, I head back to the table and set one of them down in front of Holly. "Here you go."

"Thanks."

I sit down next to her. "I always feel so useless in the gap between handing in an answer sheet and finding out who won."

"How do you deal with it when you hand in coursework?"

"Not well," I admit. "I try to choose modules that are more exam-based because of it. I hate not knowing."

"You still have to wait for exam results."

"I know. But at least I'm waiting for all of them at

the same time. At some point, there just isn't any more stress to add."

"I'm the opposite. I like having coursework because I can have more control over it before the day of the final exam. What if I get sick the day before and perform badly?"

"Hmm. Good point." And not one I thought of before. It's a new thing for me to worry about.

"The results are in," the announcer says, calling everyone's attention to him. "In third place, we have let's get quizzical."

I lean in so I can whisper to Holly. "See, I told you we didn't want to go with that one."

"You have a point."

"In second place, we have team name."

She groans. "That one's even worse."

"See, no originality."

"And in first place, we have Cholly."

"That's us!" she cries out, clearly excited by the fact we've won.

The other teams clap, but I can hear them murmuring between themselves.

"Why don't you go get it and then we can find out which questions we got wrong?" she suggests.

"Do you want to dwell on those ones?"

"No, I want to make sure that next time I enter a pub quiz, I get the answers right."

I let out a hearty chuckle. I like the way she thinks. "That's an excellent point."

I get to my feet and head over to get our quiz sheet, feeling her gaze on my back as I do. I think it's safe to say this date is going well. She certainly seems at ease. Something I hope to continue on our next date.

THREE

HOLLY

I HUM to myself as I make my way into the kitchen, only stopping when I realise I've caught a little bit of Christmas fever and am humming along with Jingle Bell Rock. Why does Christmas music have to be so catchy?

Being in a good mood makes it even harder to resist the upbeat tunes.

I start making myself some coffee, hoping it'll combat the effects of the cider from the night before. I didn't even drink much of it, but my head is still pinching and there's no way I'm going to be able to get through a whole morning of lectures without a little bit of help.

The kitchen door swings open and I glance over my shoulder to find out which of my flatmates is entering the room.

My eyebrows shoot up. "Essie? What are you doing here?"

"Oh, hey, Holly, I didn't realise you'd be here."

"I live here," I point out, though as I do, I realise there's no real way for Essie to know that. "Who are you visiting?"

The blush on her cheeks tells me it's someone she doesn't want to be caught with.

"Say no more," I promise. "Your secret is safe with me."

She laughs awkwardly. "Thanks."

"Do you want some coffee?"

"Please, I didn't get much sleep last night."

There's no stopping the knowing smile spreading over my face. I'm sure she realises I know what she's been up to. The only question remaining is which of my flatmates she's been visiting. She doesn't see to have a preference, so it could be any of the.

I grab a second mug and pour the water over the instant mix. "It's not the fanciest stuff."

"That's not a problem. I'm probably not supposed

to say this, but I honestly can't tell the difference unless it's super fancy stuff."

"Me neither. And I can't say I drink it for the taste anyway." I finish off making the coffee and hand her one.

"Thanks. So what's got you in such a good mood?" she asks as we take a seat at the kitchen table.

"Who says I'm in a good mood?"

"Call it a hunch." She grins over her mug, as if she's well aware of why.

"I had a date last night."

"Oh? Isn't this your first one in a while?" She waggles her eyebrows suggestively.

I chuckle. "Yes. I'm not really the dating type."

"So what was different with this one?"

"I'm not sure," I admit. "There was just something about him that made me ask him out for a drink."

"Sometimes, these things just feel right." The look in her eyes suggests it's not my situation she's thinking about right now.

"So, are you going to tell me what you're doing in my flat?" I ask, trying not to sound like I'm accusing her of anything, when really I'm just curious.

Essie sighs. "Making a terrible mistake."

"Now that I've got to ask about."

She lets out a small laugh. "I've never been the

kind of person who does friends with benefits, I'd rather just have a meaningless one night fling and then move on. But I just can't seem to stop falling back into bed with Byron. I'm not even sure why. It's not serious or anything."

"Sometimes you just need to have a bit of fun."

"Maybe, but I can see it blowing up in my face. Maybe I'm wrong and he'll surprise me, but until then, I'm going to keep having my fun."

"And you should," I agree.

My phone starts to buzz and I pull it out of my pocket in case it's something I need to deal with.

"Your date from last night?" Essie asks.

"Yes, actually."

< Hey, Holly, I had a great time last night. If you're free tomorrow, I'd love to take you on another date. >

A silly grin spreads over my face.

"He made quite the impression it seems." Essie sips on her coffee.

"He did."

"Was he that good of a kisser?"

A blush spreads over my cheeks. "I wouldn't know. We didn't kiss. He was a gentleman all night."

"And you think it went well?"

I nod. "I'm sure it did. And he's asked me on a second date already." I turn it around to show her.

I'm not sure why I'm suddenly being so open with her. Maybe it's because I don't really have anyone else to talk to about this, and it's not like we aren't friendly with one another. We've spent enough time in one another's company in the Fae Society.

"Oh, that's good. You should say yes."

I nod and type out my reply, hitting send without thinking about it for too long. Another date with Chris sounds perfect.

"Done. I wonder what he has planned."

"I hope it's something fun."

"I'm sure it will be."

Essie checks her own phone and groans. "I need to go. If I don't leave now, I won't be able to shower before Spanish. I'll see you there?"

"Hopefully I'll be able to get rid of my mini hangover by then," I respond.

"Oh yes, I can't imagine that'll be fun when we're meant to be conjugating verbs."

"Hopefully, it'll be something easy so I don't have to concentrate too much on it."

"You and me both." She gets to her feet and hands me the coffee mug. "Thank you for the coffee."

"Any time, the one at the end is my cupboard, help yourself next time you're here." I don't ask why Byron isn't making her morning drinks. They must not be at that stage yet. If I get the chance, I'll start dropping hints about it.

She waves goodbye, leaving me alone in the kitchen. I down the rest of my coffee so I can go get ready for class. It may not make a difference whether or not we show up, but I came to Obscure Academy because I want to learn, which means going to my lectures unless I have a good reason not to.

And it's not like it can put much of a damper on my mood. Tomorrow can't come soon enough.

FOUR

HOLLY

THE BRIGHT LIGHTS, cheerful atmosphere, and the scent of delicious food all fill the air with a sense of merriment that I have to admit is endearing, even if I don't want to.

"Bringing me to a Christmas market was a bit of a risk," I tell Chris, being careful not to put any annoyance into my voice. I don't really mind, it's nicer than I expected.

"I even wore a Christmas jumper." He pulls open his coat to show me a cream jumper complete with a seasonal pattern.

"It's not the worst one I've ever seen."

"But it's close, right?"

I let out a soft snort. "Are you purposefully wearing a jumper for me to hate on?"

"Maybe. I thought you could destroy it at the end of the night if you were still feeling like you wanted to uphold your bah, humbug approach to Christmas."

"I'm not that bad," I mutter.

"Not from what I've seen, no." He directs us towards a stall selling hot chocolate in cute mugs. "What would you like?"

"What's good?"

"Everything. You can have a hot chocolate plain, or you can have it with brandy, spiced rum, anything you want."

"Rum sounds good, I'll have one of those." The spices will go well with the richness of the chocolate. I think. I'm not actually a hundred per cent sure about that, I've never tried it.

Chris turns away from me and orders for us. It only takes the woman behind the counter a few minutes to produce two steaming hot chocolates.

"How do they make any money if they serve all the drinks in proper mugs?" I wrap my hands around the mug, enjoying the warmth that seeps into me from it.

"They take a deposit. You return your mug to one

of the stalls before you go and you get your money back. Or you can keep the mug."

"That's an interesting system."

"It's much better than using disposable cups everywhere. My sister has a collection of Christmas market mugs at home, she gets a new one for every market she visits."

"She must really love Christmas." This time, the bitterness does manage to seep through. I know I should do a better job of keeping my feelings about the time of year to myself, but I can't help it.

Besides, the honesty that seems to already be part of whatever is between me and Chris is one of my favourite parts of whatever this is.

We make our way over to one of the benches and sit on it, close enough that we're almost touching. I take a sip of my hot chocolate, pleasantly surprised by how delicious it is when mixed with the spiced rum. I'd never have thought to add it, but I might have to change that.

"Why don't you like Christmas?" he asks.

"Wow, you're going in for the big revelations right away," I observe.

"It's the elephant in the room."

"We're outside."

He chuckles. "Then it's the elephant in the street."

"I'm not sure that has the same effect."

"There are a lot of people around, an elephant would be a bit of a problem."

"Fair point," I concede.

"You don't have to answer if you don't want," he assures me.

"It's fine. I guess I've not been very subtle about it." I take a deep breath. I've never really talked to anyone about this. Not because I don't want anyone to know, but no one has ever asked and it's not the kind of thing I've ever really wanted to raise with anyone. "When I was little, the other kids in the playground used to tease me a lot about being an elf. They thought I'd be able to get them better presents at Christmas or something like that. It was never very clear."

"And that made you hate this time of year?"

I nod. "It was always worse around the holidays, and I started dreading going to school and social events, and I guess it kind of stuck, even once I was in secondary school and it kind of wore off."

"I'm sorry they were so cruel," Chris says softly.

"It's not your fault, I'm sure you've dealt with something similar."

"Maybe a comment or two, but nothing to that extent. But I wasn't the only elf in school, so I suspect that helped."

"Ah." That explains it. "It's not necessarily the

Christmas stuff I don't like. A lot of it's fun, especially the food."

"You're not wrong there," he agrees.

"And I like spending time with the people I care about."

"Hence why you're doing Secret Santa."

"Mmhmm. But I guess this time of year puts me a little on edge because of everything I've been through already, and that's hard to get past, even if people are nicer about it now."

He nods. "I understand. And if this is too much for you, just say so and we can do something else."

"No, this is nice," I admit. "There's something oddly peaceful about sitting and drinking hot chocolate while surrounded by so many people."

"I know what you mean."

We lapse into comfortable silence as we finish our drinks.

"So, what's next on our tour of the Christmas market?" I ask.

"That depends, are you hungry or do you want to go ice skating?"

"Food is always going to win."

An amused laugh escapes from him. "That's a fair point. Sweet or savoury?"

"Both. Always both."

"That sounds good to me. Do you want to take a

walk around and pick out what we want? Then we can come back and eat it all?"

"Or even take it back to the dorms if it gets much colder."

"Smart. It looks like it might rain too."

I glance up at the sky, unsurprised to find dark clouds rolling across it.

"If you give me your mug, I can put it in my handbag until we get another drink?" I suggest.

"Are you sure?"

I nod. "There isn't much else in there."

He hands me his mug and I slip both of them inside my bag, glad I brought it in the end. I considered leaving it back in my room, but thought better of it.

We head out into the market, and I let the sights and sounds of it wash over me. There really is something great about the market, though I don't know what it is.

Perhaps it's the company.

Chris' hand bumps against mine and I take the chance to slip my hand into his and entwine our fingers together. He doesn't pull away. In fact, he glances at me with a smile on his face, which only makes me more comfortable with the situation.

There's something easy about spending time with Chris. He makes me feel as if none of the bad stuff matters, there's always going to be a way to get past it.

"So, I had a question for you," he says once we've made a few purchases. My bag is getting a little heavy now, though I refuse to let him carry it for me.

"Okay?"

"How would you feel if I asked whether I can kiss you?"

My heart flutters in response to his question. "I'd be favourable to it. Is there anywhere in particular you had in mind?"

He grins and tugs on my hand, pulling me into a sheltered part of the market away from the prying eyes of the other people spending their time there.

My gaze locks with his, and I'm unable to deny the intensity within his eyes. I'm sure mine look the same.

He reaches out and brushes a strand of dark-brown hair away from my face, his touch leaving tingles against my skin.

"You can say no," he whispers.

"I don't want to," I assure him. "I want you to kiss me."

He steps forward and snakes a hand around my waist, pressing a hand against my lower back and using it to pull me closer.

I go willingly, not wanting to prolong the sweet torture of waiting for him to kiss me.

The moment his lips touch mine, every thought disappears from my mind. The only thing I'm able to focus on is the slight taste of the hot chocolate we drank, and the way he's pressed against me. It's a connection I don't have the words to describe, like things are snapping into place and becoming what they're meant to be.

It feels like a romanticised version of the way I want a relationship to start, but I'm not making it up. There's no denying that there is something between us and it can't be ignored.

We pull apart, both breathing raggedly.

"Wow," I whisper.

He chuckles deeply. "That's one way of putting it."

"I wouldn't mind doing that again," I respond.

"Me neither."

"I'm definitely going to advocate going back to the dorms once we've finished food shopping."

He raises an eyebrow, his surprise written all over his face.

"Not for that," I say quickly, a blush rising to my cheeks.

"Sorry," he mutters.

"I just mean that it'll be nice to spend some time

just the two of us. Our dates have been very public so far."

"You're not wrong. But I didn't want you to feel pressured by being more one-on-one."

"That's sweet." I lean in and kiss him swiftly again.

A content smile spreads over his face. "All right, then let's go finish buying ourselves some food and then we'll head back to one of our flats to have a small feast."

"That sounds good to me." And I'm not lying, even if his plan does involve spending more time around something overtly Christmassy.

I'm finding I don't mind it nearly as much as I thought I would.

FIVE

HOLLY

I SIGH DREAMILY as I make my way back into my flat. I'm a little sad that my date with Chris is over, but that only means that we get to plan our next one.

Loud shouts come from down the hallway, and I duck to the side in time to avoid Byron running straight into me.

"What's going on?" I ask.

"We're playing a game of assassin." He slurs his words a little, suggesting they've been drinking.

I'd probably be playing along with them if I'd been here already.

"Have fun." I pat him on the arm and head down to my room and the safety of not playing the game.

I slip inside and close the door behind me, not bothering to lock it. There's no point when I'm not sleeping or gone, it only creates an annoyance when I want to leave to make myself a drink.

I pull out my phone and type out a message.

< I had a great time tonight even if it was a Christmas date! >

Chris' reply comes quickly, as if he's been waiting for me to send it.

< It was a lot of fun. Can't wait to do it again. >

< Soon? > The message is sent before I can think twice about whether it could be seen as too needy to send it.

< As soon as you want. >

Satisfaction floods through me and it's all I can do not twirl around and flop onto my bed like some kind of love-struck princess in a movie.

I've never felt this way about anyone before, and it's making me feel a little light-headed. Or at least I think it's that, I didn't drink any alcohol other than the small drop in my hot chocolate at the beginning of the night, and I ate more than enough carbs to soak that up.

My door bursts open and Hannah barges in.

"I need to hide," she announces.

"Assassin?" I guess.

She nods.

"I don't think my room is a safe zone," I point out.

"Yes, but do people know you're in?"

"Byron does."

"Then I'd better get going." She pulls open the door and rushes out, only to end up stumbling back when Byron moves into the room brandishing a ruler while he pretends to try and assassinate her for the game.

She waves her arms around, bringing them worryingly close to the desk where my laptop and Secret Santa gift are sitting.

"Whoa," I shout as she starts to fall towards it. I hold out my arms to try and steady her before she hurts herself, but it's too late for the gift basket of soap.

Hannah's flailing arm knocks it to the ground and I can only watch in horror as one of the softer bars disintegrates and spills all over my floor.

At least Hannah has managed to regain her feet.

"Oh, Holly, I'm sorry, I didn't mean to..."

"It's fine," I cut her off. "It's only a gift. It's not a big deal." It's going to be a pain to clean up, but at least it's not my laptop. That could have been a lot more of a disaster, especially if it had broken.

"Sorry, Holly," Byron murmurs.

"It's fine, I promise. I'll just clean it up and it'll be as if it never happened."

"At least let us pay for a replacement," Hannah says.

I pause for a moment, unsure if I want to say yes. I know Hannah isn't being supported by her parents while she studies and I don't want to add to that.

"It's fine, it wasn't expensive. Are you okay? That's the main thing," I assure her.

"I'll probably have a bruise, but I think I'm okay," she says.

"You should both go finish your game. My room is now out of bounds though." I don't want to deal with more drunken flatmates causing potential problems for me. I know it's not their fault, especially as I've joined in their games before. They have no reason to think I don't want to take part today either.

"If you have any problems cleaning up, let us know," Byron says.

"I'll be fine." I don't think it'll take too much doing, and it's soap anyway, how much harm can that do?

The two of them exchange an uneasy look, as if they don't want to leave me to it, but they also want to return to their game.

"Go," I insist.

"Thanks, Holly," Hannah says as the two of them leave the room.

The moment they're gone, I let out a loud sigh. This isn't what I needed. I'll have to go back to Aroma to get a replacement gift basket, but that's not necessarily the worst thing when it means I may be able to talk to Chris, even if it's just for five minutes.

I rescue what I can of the gift basket and relocate it to my bathroom. It's not my preferred scent, but I'm not going to waste decent products.

All I need to do now is get the crumbs of soap off the floor, hopefully, it's not going to be too hard to do. Though I may need the vacuum which is sadly on the other side of the door along with my warring flatmates. I'm not foolish enough to think that they'll have stopped because of one small accident.

I briefly consider messaging Chris and asking him if he can put another basket aside for me, but I dismiss the notion. There were plenty of them the other day, I doubt it's going to be a problem. And I don't want him to think I'm using him for his position at work.

My afternoon is free tomorrow, I'll just go down to the store and pick up a replacement.

This isn't the end to my date that I wanted or expected, but it could be a lot worse.

SIX

HOLLY

THERE AREN'T as many people around as there were the first day I came to Aroma. Perhaps it's because it's three in the afternoon on a Wednesday and most people have already finished their Christmas shopping.

I'm not naive enough to think that's true. There are plenty of people who will leave it even more last-minute than a few weeks before the big day.

I make a beeline for Aroma, not seeing any real need to dally for longer than necessary. If I get in and out, then I'll have plenty of time to do other things with my day as well as run an errand.

"Good afternoon, welcome to Aroma, how can I help you?" a cheery woman says as I enter.

Disappointment wells up within me as I realise it isn't Chris greeting me at the door.

"I'm fine, thank you. I know what I want."

"Excellent. If you change your mind and need assistance, please let me or one of the other sales reps know and we'll be happy to help." She smiles widely, but it's easily recognisable as a customer service smile. She doesn't mean it. Not in the way Chris does.

I'm becoming a one-track record even inside my own head. I know it'll die down once the two of us establish what we're going to be to one another.

I ignore my thoughts and head to the back of the store where we got the Tutti Frutti basket from before.

My heart sinks as I take in the gaps on the shelf where the smallest size should be. Why isn't it there? The other sizes still are.

I double-check the shelves on either side to see if it's been put in the wrong place, but don't see anything. I let out a loud sigh. I guess I'm going to have to talk to one of the sales reps after all.

A young woman with a bored expression on her face stands not far away from me. She's the one I'm going to have to talk to, even if her face looks like thunder.

I start to head towards her, but the glare I receive in response is enough to put me off. I change directions and go back to the front of the store where the cheerier woman had been situated.

"Hi, do you need some help after all?" she asks with her false smile.

"Yes, please. I bought a small Tutti Frutti gift basket from here the other day and I was looking to get another one, but I can't find it on the shelves. Are there any in the back?"

"I don't think so. Most of our gift baskets are out on display. But I can go check if you give me a moment."

"Thanks, I'd appreciate that, I really want to get another one."

She nods. "I'll be back in a moment." She disappears through a door behind the tills, presumably to try and find the gift basket in the back.

I glance around, wondering what I'm supposed to do with myself while I wait for her. That's not particularly clear. I resist the urge to pull my phone out and start messing with it in case she comes back and thinks I've lost interest in what I've asked for.

After what feels like an age, she reappears empty-handed.

That's not a good sign. I can't buy an invisible gift basket, and I need a Secret Santa gift or I'm going to be in serious trouble once our flat Christmas dinner comes around.

Or maybe not. The whole idea of Secret Santa is that the giver remains a secret, but I don't think that's how it ever works in practice. People like to guess who got which present.

Which means that I have to get a present and it has to be a good one.

"I'm really sorry, we're completely out of the small Tutti Fruitti gift basket. There is the medium, that one is twelve pounds..."

"I'm sorry, that's out of my gift price range."

She flashes me a false smile. "You could try our website."

Oh, why didn't I think of that?

"How long does shipping take?"

"Two to three days normally," she responds. "But I think it's longer around Christmas."

Of course it is. Being able to get things quickly would make everything too easy.

"Okay, thank you for looking." I force a smile to my face, though I imagine it looks about as real as hers does. "I hope you enjoy the rest of your day."

"You too, thank you for shopping at Aroma."

I nod as I turn away, frustrated that my search for the perfect Secret Santa gift has been thwarted by a game of assassin.

I make my way out of Aroma and stand in the middle of the shopping centre, scanning the shops around me while trying to work out which of them is most likely to have a Grace appropriate gift inside. It's frustrating because I've had the perfect idea, I stopped thinking after I decided on it, which is a bit of a problem when I can't get it.

I suppose I could get a few other things and make up my own gift basket to replace the items that broke. One look on the Aroma website would reveal what I'd done, but that's not necessarily a bad thing.

Maybe.

I take a deep breath. Standing here and mulling things over isn't going to find me the perfect replacement gift. While I'd much rather go into a shop with the existing knowledge about what I want to get there, I need to get moving. Maybe something will catch my eye and give me an idea.

With the long shipping from ordering online, and the shop having run out of what I want, I don't see that I have any other choice.

I set off towards the nearest shop, hoping that I'll be able to find something just right inside it, and almost dreading what will happen if I don't. The last thing I want is for someone to end up with a sub-par gift, especially when the whole point of doing Secret Santa was so that people got something a little bit better.

Chris' flatmates' pound Secret Santa idea is looking particularly appealing right now. At least with a joke present, it's not possible to go too wrong, even for someone like Grace.

But considering what could have been is no use. I need to focus on solving the actual problem at hand, and not the fake situations I'm making up myself.

SEVEN

CHRIS

I TURN the corner in the shopping centre to find a familiar figure slumped on one of the benches. Panic sets in as I consider the possibilities that could have led to Holly being hurt, but she moves just enough for me to see that she's okay.

"Holly? What are you doing here?" I ask.

She looks up, her gaze locking on me and relief flooding her features when she realises it's me.

I like it. Kind of. I don't like that she seems down, but I do like that she seems happy to see me.

"Hey," she says.

I sit on the bench beside her. "Why do you look so down?"

"My flatmates broke my Secret Santa gift."

"That's annoying." Especially when she seemed so pleased with it when we met in Aroma.

"It's not the worst bit. I came to buy a replacement, but Aroma said that there weren't any more of the small ones."

"Ah. And your dinner is too soon to order from the website?" I ask.

"Right you are."

"I'm sorry," I say.

"Don't be. It's not your fault my flatmates got drunk." She sounds so defeated. I wish there was something I could do about it.

"Yeah, that's not great."

"And now I need to find a replacement gift." She rubs her sleeve over her face. "I'm not doing very well."

"I can tell."

She lets out a loud sigh. "I don't know what to get her. I had this perfect idea and now it's all ruined."

"Do you want me to go check if the assistant you asked was telling the truth about them being out of stock?"

"I'm sure they were."

"But I can go check the stock room. Maybe one

got placed wrong." It's happened plenty of times before.

"If you want..."

"I will if you give me a tenner."

A dry chuckle comes from her, but she pulls the money from her pocket and hands it to me anyway. "You're lucky I haven't completely converted to using a bank card."

"You shouldn't. They can't be trusted."

"What a fae thing for you to say."

"We are fae," I point out. "Well, a kind of fae."

"True. But it's also an old-fashioned thing to say."

"Maybe I'm an old-fashioned kind of fae." I'm not sure what makes me say it.

She raises an eyebrow. "Are you?"

I lean in and kiss her cheek instead of answering. She's already made her mind up about the kind of fae I am. I wouldn't have a job at Aroma if I was the old-fashioned kind.

"Don't move, I'll be back."

"Even a finger?" she attempts to joke.

"Huh?"

"You said don't move. Does that mean I can't even move a finger?" She wiggles them back and forth.

Amusement fills me. "What would you do if I said no?"

"I'm not really sure," she admits. "Try to keep

them still as part of the challenge but probably fail miserably at it."

"That's fair. I'd probably do the same. But I just mean that I'll be right back."

I turn and head to the shop, knowing that I need to be quick if I don't want her to end up too down. But I have a plan. One I'm not sure she'd have agreed to if I told her beforehand, but as I'm not going to go above the ten-pound limit they have, I don't think she'll mind.

I hurry into the shop and locate the right basket of Tutti Frutti, pay and leave to find her still on the bench twiddling her thumbs.

A small smile lifts at my lips as I realise she's moving a finger after all. I hope she's getting as much amusement out of that fact as I am.

Her face lights up when she sees me, though maybe it's for the bag in my hands instead.

I sit back down on the bench next to her and hold out the bag. "Problem solved."

"There was one in the back?" she asks hopefully.

"Not exactly," I admit.

She pulls open the bag, letting out a whiff of Tutti Frutti. I have to admit, it isn't quite as potent out here as it is in the shop.

"This is the medium-sized one? I can't give her

this, it's over the budget." Disappointment comes through her voice.

"Ah, I thought you'd say that. I present you with proof that it's still under ten pounds." I hand her the receipt, trying not to feel too satisfied about my clever use of discounts.

She takes it from me and scans it for the information she needs. "Ah, staff discount."

"Exactly. I believe my twenty per cent discount actually leaves you with forty pence left to spend." A satisfied grin spreads over my face. "I think that's what they call a loophole." And all fae love a good loop-hole, even if they're not old-fashioned.

"Thank you." She leans in.

I turn my head without realising what she's doing, and our lips meet. It only takes a moment for me to put the pieces together, but I'm glad that I get to kiss her again. It isn't quite the next kiss I had in mind, but so long as there is one, I don't see how it's a problem.

She cups my cheek in her hand, and I pull her closer, deepening our kiss. I can't think of anything other than Holly and the way it feels to connect with her like this. I'm not sure exactly what's different about the elf in front of me, but something is. Kissing her is unlike anything I've experienced before.

We break apart, and I don't miss the wide grin on Holly's face. Her mood has completely shifted.

"Please tell me you're free now?" she asks.

"Luckily for you, I just came to pick up a present I ordered for Mum. So long as we pick that up, I'm at your service," I respond.

"That sounds good."

"What did you have in mind?" I ask.

"I wouldn't mind going back to the Christmas market."

I raise an eyebrow, surprised by her choice, but not against it. "I thought you didn't like Christmas."

"It's not Christmas itself I have a problem with," she admits. "The food tastes good, and I like getting to spend time with people, but the forced cheeriness and the way everyone is supposed to act happy around everyone. But I think I can sort of understand why people like it so much now."

"Oh?"

She lets out a loud sigh. "It's hard to explain. But it's been a lot of fun exploring the Christmas markets and trying all the different food. And I guess it helped me see a different side of the season. I could get used to it."

"Ah, that makes sense. If you want to continue your Christmas is fun education, we could do something," I suggest.

"What did you have in mind?"

"I take it going to visit the elves at Santa's grotto is out of the question?"

"That might be a step too far," she agrees.

"Fair. We could go ice skating, or we could catch a movie?"

"That last one sounds good. I can think of some fun ways to pass the time in the dark if I don't like the movie."

I clear my throat. "That sounds very enjoyable."

"Then let's go get your Mum's present and then head to the cinema?"

I get to my feet and hold out my hand for her. She takes it, our fingers entwining perfectly together.

"Thank you for helping me with Grace's present," she says.

"You're welcome."

"Movie tickets on me?"

"If you insist, but I'm buying the popcorn." It should always be a fair trade.

"It sounds like a date."

Yes, it does. And I hope it's the next of many.

EIGHT

HOLLY

I PULL the chicken out of the oven and place it on the chopping board. We've misjudged the timings and it won't have long to rest, but I don't think that matters too much. Considering we're all students and this is being done on a budget so lean there's no turkey, I don't think any of us are expecting a gourmet meal.

"Will you put it on the table?" I ask Byron.

"Sure." He picks it up and takes it over to join the steaming plates of vegetables.

The kitchen is packed, as it's going to be with all nine of us in it. We're normally only in the same room together when there's an event on and we all want to pre-drink, but that's a little different to having a meal.

A tiny pound shop Christmas tree sits in the corner with our gifts beneath it.

Even a week or two ago, I'd be feeling resentful towards the set-up, but with Chris' help, I'm starting to see things more clearly and I'm actually looking forward to spending some time with my flatmates.

"Where's Grace?" Hannah asks.

"I think she has cheer practice," Byron answers.

"On the last week of term?" I set a bowl of stuffing down.

He shrugs. "I think there's a game tomorrow, they're getting some last-minute practice in."

"Ah."

As if summoned by the mention of her name, Grace tumbles through the door, still wearing her cheerleading outfit. "Sorry, sorry, the captain wouldn't stop talking about how she expects us all to keep up our exercise regimes over the holidays." Grace grimaces. "As if she thinks I'm going to skip Grandma's Christmas pudding."

"We have a cake for after today too," Byron says.

"I might have to pass on that," Grace responds, dropping into the only empty chair. "I still have to go and cheer on the football team tomorrow." She grimaces.

"I thought you liked cheering?" I ask.

"I do, but I much prefer it when the basketball team plays, they actually win."

Byron chuckles. "Don't you mean you like watching Fabio drop hoops?"

A furious blush sneaks across Grace's face. "No," she mumbles. "This all looks delicious. Why don't we dig in?"

I raise an eyebrow at her attempt to divert attention away from herself.

"We should pull our crackers first," Dean puts in, picking up his Christmas cracker and waving it in Kerry's face.

She takes the other end of it without much protest and tugs on it. A sharp crack fills the air as the cracker breaks in two and spills the paper hat, plastic toy, and cracker joke.

Kerry picks up the joke and clears her throat. "What did the sea say to Santa?"

"Oh, I know this," Dean mutters even as he puts on the paper hat from his cracker.

"Nothing, it just waved," Kerry finishes.

I let out a small groan, as do several of the others around the table. Christmas cracker jokes are in a league of their own for how bad they are.

Hannah presents her cracker to me, and we pull

it before switching to do mine. I put my paper hat on with surprisingly little reluctance.

Inspiration strikes and I pull out my phone to take a selfie to send to Chris. I even make sure my ears are showing on it.

< Having Christmas dinner with my flatmates and getting into the spirit of things! >

I hit send before I can think too much about it.

"Hey, no we said no phones," Hannah admonishes me.

"I know, I know. I just had to send a picture to someone."

"The guy you've been seeing?" Grace asks.

"Erm..." How do I answer that one? I slip my phone into my pocket. I'll message Chris more later.

"Oh, the cute guy you were with at the Christmas market the other day?" Hannah puts in.

"I didn't see you." Did she say hi and I ignored her?

"It was just a glimpse. I was there with my family."

"Ah."

"You seemed to be having a good time," she says.

"We were," I agree. "I'm seeing him again tomorrow." I start loading up my plate before everything goes cold and let the general chatter that doesn't concern me and Chris overtake me. All of us have our own groups of friends and only hang out with one another on occasion, but it's nice to have everyone around the same table so we can all catch up.

The scrape of knives and forks against empty plates soon fills the air and no one says anything. Which is impressive when there are nine of us around the table.

Byron leans back in his chair, letting out a satisfied groan. "That was good. Probably the best food I've eaten all term."

"That's because you normally eat crap all day," Hannah reminds him. "I saw you dipping chicken nuggets in cream cheese the other day."

"It's tasty, you should try it."

"I think I'll pass."

"Maybe we should do Secret Santa before we have dessert?" Dean suggests.

"Good idea. I don't think I could eat another bite right now," Hannah agrees, getting up and making her way over to the Christmas tree to hand out presents.

She's not wrong. I'm stuffed from all the food. Unsurprisingly, there isn't much left after all of us have eaten our fill.

"Here you go, Holly," she says as she hands me a squidgy parcel. "Grace, Byron, Georgie..." She hands each of the people around the table the parcel with their name on it before retaking her seat.

"So now what do we do?" Grace asks. "All at once, or take turns?"

Hannah groans. "All at once, please. My grandparents make us all watch each other open our presents and it's always so awkward."

"All right, all together then," Grace says. "Ready?"

Everyone voices their agreement and starts ripping into their presents.

I watch Grace out of the corner of my eye, even as I pull the paper from my own gift. I have to admit, I'm more curious than I thought I'd be by what's inside and how well one of the people around the table knows me.

"These are amazing," Hannah says, holding up a pack of fun socks while grinning. It's a good present, she's always wearing mismatched socks with bright patterns.

Byron chuckles. "I don't even know what this is." He holds up a box with a circular contraption on the front of it.

Hannah leans in and frowns. "I think it's supposed to be for making whisky ice."

"Oh. Neat."

I frown. Does he even drink whisky? I've never paid enough attention to what he drinks. I should change that. Maybe I'm a bad flatmate for not paying enough attention.

I finish removing the paper from mine revealing a wide knit scarf that's so soft, I want to rub my face on it. "Thank you, it's beautiful," I say to whoever my Secret Santa is. I wrap it around my neck despite the warmth in the room. It's cosy, and just what I need in the cold.

Grace gives a small squeak. "I love this stuff." She beams. "And I'm running short, I was hoping I'd get some for Christmas," she babbles.

Pride wells up within me for making a good choice. And for making sure I went back to get another one.

Hannah side-eyes me, clearly making the connection between the gift Grace has just opened, and the gift basket she and Byron destroyed the other day.

I just smile at her, but don't say anything. It doesn't really matter if she knows that I got Grace, especially as the recipient of my gift seems more than pleased with it. If she finds out it's me that got it for her, it's not the end of the world.

"Are we supposed to reveal who we got now?" Bryon asks.

"No, it's got to remain a secret," Grace insists.

Maybe she's the person behind the whisky ice ball and doesn't want it to come out.

Everyone exchanges their expressions of gratitude, though it's a little odd when no one quite knows who to direct it to.

Torn gift wrap litters the floor of the kitchen, along with the remnants of our crackers. It's going to be a pain to clear up, though thankfully I don't think I'll have to do that thanks to the amount I did to make the dinner in the first place.

Satisfied that everyone is busy talking among themselves, I slip my phone back out of my pocket to see if Chris has messaged me back. A small smile spreads over my face as I realise he has.

< Looks like you're having fun! Did Grace like her present? >

< She did! Loved it. Thanks for helping me with it! >

I shut it off and put it away before helping to clear the table so we can do dessert. I have to admit, for Christmas dinner, it's been a lot of fun.

NINE

HOLLY

I BOUNCE DOWN THE HALLWAY, filled with excitement about the prospect of seeing the person on the other side of the door. I pull it open and usher Chris inside.

"So this is where you live?" he asks. "It looks just like where I do."

I snort. "Your flat is laid out in the opposite direction."

"So different."

I let out a small laugh. "There are Christmas dinner sandwiches ready for us. I used the leftovers from our dinner." I draw him towards the kitchen.

"Are your flatmates okay with that?"

"They've all gone home for the holidays, I don't leave until tomorrow. All the leftovers are mine. I'm surprised you haven't left yet."

"I only live an hour away, it doesn't matter much when I leave."

I point to the kitchen table and head over to the side to collect our sandwiches. Maybe it's not the fanciest food for a date, but we're students and this is already paid for.

"Are you looking forward to seeing your family?" I ask.

He nods. "You?"

"Yes. And you'll be glad to know I'll be taking part in many more festive activities."

"Does that mean I'll get more cute photos of you in paper hats?"

Warmth floods through me at the thought of us continuing to message one another over the break. I've been worrying about whether the time apart will cause any problems in our budding relationship. "You have as many of them as you want."

"I'll make sure to send you just as many in return," he promises. "I nearly brought you a cracker today just so I could see it again."

"There are a couple left over from our meal," I

say, jumping to my feet and grabbing them from the side. "It'll make our sandwiches more exciting."

I hold one of them out to him and he tugs on it. The sharp crack fills the air, and the contents falls out.

"Oh, you got one of the frogs."

"The what?" Amusement dances in his voice.

"The frogs. You flick them on the tail and they jump. Watch." I pick up the small plastic frog that came in the cracker. It's cheap and cheerful, and won't have a life after today, but that's the whole point. I press down on the small tab on its bum and it jumps upwards across the table.

"I've never seen one of those before."

"What kind of Christmas crackers do you have in your house? These are some of the most popular ones."

"Oh, Mum likes to get those novelty ones where the penguins race around a track. She thinks it's more fun."

"Is it?"

"I don't know, this frog is pretty cool." He flicks it, making it jump. "What's in the other one?"

"Want to find out?" I offer it to him so we can pull it.

"What's this one?" he asks, picking up the gift.

At this rate, we're never going to get to eating our food, but I don't mind.

"What am I supposed to do with a translucent fish?" He frowns, clearly confused by the cracker's gift.

I don't know how he's going to react when we get to the jokes.

"You put it in your hand and ask it a question, if the head curls up, the answer is yes, if the tail curls up, the answer is no," I say.

"Is it accurate?"

"It came out of crackers that cost three quid, I think the answer is no."

"Not according to the fish." He grins.

"Wow, that was bad."

"Let me try it." He takes the fish out of the packet and places it onto his hand. "Hmm, what to ask it."

"Do you tell the truth?" I suggest.

"Oh no, I have a better one." He clears his throat. "Oh magic fish, will Holly go on another date with me once term starts again?"

The head of the fish bobs up.

"So, does it tell the truth?" There's a hopeful expression on his face, but he isn't acting as if it's a sure thing.

"It does."

"Excellent." He sets the fish down and passes me the hat, and takes the other one for himself.

I unfold mine and place it on my head, trying not to tear it in the process. "Now we're really ready for our meal," I announce.

"Only after we've taken a picture." He shuffles down the bench and I take it as an invitation to sit next to him.

I get up and make my way over to him. Our legs brush against one another as he puts his arm around me and holds his phone up to take the picture. I smile, genuinely, enjoying the moment and glad we get to capture it.

"Send it to me?" I ask once he's done.

"I'm already on it." He sets his phone down and turns towards me.

I bite my bottom lip, hoping he's going to lean in and kiss me.

Much to my relief he reaches out and tucks a strand of hair behind my ear.

My eyes flutter closed as his lips press against mine and I melt into him. Everything about it makes me certain that there'll be something between us once the festive season is over and the two of us return to the academy.

I don't think anyone's going to believe that I started to date someone while everything is all dressed up for Christmas, but it doesn't matter. Everything happens for a reason, and maybe I met Chris just in time to teach me that I don't have to always hold to the past and I can enjoy the season and all the fun it brings with them.

I pull away from him just as my stomach starts to grumble. It's time to eat, no matter how much more fun kissing is.

"I look forward to our next date."

Chris smiles at me. "I do too."

I can barely keep the smile from my face, and I have no need to. This has been my best Christmas in years.

THANK you for reading Secret Santa For Grumpy Elves, I hope you enjoyed it! If you want to discover more fae antics at Obscure Academy, then you can with Trading Names For Polite Sprites, featuring Essie & Byron: http://books2read.com/ tradingnamesforpolitesprites (Grace will also get her own book later in the series!)

You can also get Holly's point of view for chapters 2 & 7 for free here: https://books. authorlauragreenwood.co.uk/9kprrt12t4

AUTHOR NOTE

Thank you for reading Secret Santa For Grumpy Elves, I hope you enjoyed it!

While I did plan in a Christmas themed book for 2021 anyway (The Reindeer's Spell, part of the Paranormal Council series), it's always fun to come up with ideas later in the year, and that's what Secret Santa For Grumpy Elves is - a story that wouldn't leave me until I wrote it. I do hope to add more holiday stories, but they'll all be surprise releases, so keep an eye on my Facebook Reader Group or Mailing List to stay up to date on them!

Obscure Academy, and some of the antics from this book, is loosely inspired by my own time at university and the friends I was lucky enough to make there. Like Chris' flatmates did, my own group of friends used to do Poundland Secret Santa. We'd have a pound as a budget and we'd need to go to one of the many pound shops (everything in the shops was a pound) that filled Birmingham (UK) at the time to pick out a present - the funnier the better! I really did get a toy kitchen one year (but not because I was bad at cooking, just because my flatmate always wanted to help in the kitchen and I said no because she liked to drop things), honourable mentions have to go to the toy dinosaurs received because one of my flatmates had a hungover breakdown about the fact she wasn't a dinosaur, a toy phone for the friend who constantly lost hers (eight in one year, we had a spare number saved for her), and the "excavate your own dinosaur bones" kit for a friend who announced that they didn't believe dinosaurs were real (worryingly, she is now a teacher!) We had a lot of fun, and I really hope that comes across in the Obscure Academy antics!

Thank you to the readers who provided me with the Pub Quiz questions! Samantha Y. for the Canadian maple syrup heist worth $18 million, Savannah B. for the male seahorse being the one to carry young, and Rebecca W. for the man eating the Cessna 150 plane! And if you want to know who the last king of France was, it was Louis Philippe I (I was paying attention in my France since the revolution module!)

As a side note: while some of the antics, fun events, and other aspects are based on my time at university, none of the characters are based on my friends - I'd rather keep my wedding invitations!

If you want to keep up to date with new releases and other news, you can join my Facebook Reader Group or mailing list.

Stay safe & happy reading!

- Laura

The Forgotten Gods World

A fantasy romance world based on Egyptian mythology.
Each series can be read on its own, but there are cameos
from past characters and mentions of previous events.

Forgotten Gods - The Queen of Gods* - Forgotten Gods:
Origins*

* * *

The Egyptian Empire

A modern fantasy world set in an alternative timeline
where the Egyptian Empire never fell.

The Apprentice Of Anubis

* * *

The Paranormal Council World

A paranormal romance & urban fantasy world where
paranormals are hidden away from the human world, and
are in search of their fated mates. Each series can be read

on its own, but there are cameos from past characters and mentions of previous events.

The Paranormal Council Series* - The Fae Queens* - Paranormal Criminal Investigations* - The Necromancer Council* - Return Of The Fae*

Other Series

Purple Oasis (with Arizona Tape) - Grimm Academy - Beyond The Curse* - Untold Tales* - The Dragon Duels* - Speed Dating With The Denizens Of The Underworld (shared world) - Seven Wardens* (with Skye MacKinnon) - Tales Of Clan Robbins (co-written with L.A. Boruff) - Firehouse Witches* (with Lacey Carter Andersen & L.A. Boruff) - Valentine Pride* (with Lainie Anderson) - Magic and Metaphysics Academy* (with Lainie Anderson)

Twin Souls Universe

A paranormal romance & urban fantasy world co-written with Arizona Tape. Each series can be read on its own, but there are cameos from past characters and mentions of previous events.

Amethyst's Wand Shop Mysteries - Twin Souls* - The Vampire Detective*

ABOUT LAURA GREENWOOD

Laura is a USA Today Bestselling Author of paranormal, fantasy, urban fantasy, and contemporary romance. When she's not writing, she drinks a lot of tea, tries to resist French macarons, and works towards a diploma in Egyptology. She lives in the UK, where most of her books are set. Laura specialises in quick reads, whether you're looking for a swoonworthy romance for the bath, or an action-packed adventure for your latest journey, you'll find the perfect match amongst her books!

Follow the Author

- Website: www.authorlauragreenwood.co.uk
- Mailing List: www.authorlauragreenwood.co.uk/p/mailing-list-sign-up.html
- Facebook Group: http://facebook.com/groups/theparanormalcouncil

- Facebook Page: http://facebook.com/authorlauragreenwood
- Bookbub: www.bookbub.com/authors/laura-greenwood